Scan the QR code
to read and listen to the
glossary words for FREE!

glossary - *Meanings of words.*

Dados Internacionais de Catalogação na Publicação (CIP) de acordo com ISBD

C319a Carroll, Lewis
Alice's adventures in Wonderland - Easier Classics Reading / Lewis Carroll. – Jandira : W. Books, 2025.
200 p. ; 12,8cm x 19,8cm. – (Easier Classics Reading Library Children's Collection)

ISBN: 978-65-5294-161-9

1. Literatura infantojuvenil. 2. Literatura Infantil. 3. Clássicos. 4. Aventura. 5. Imaginação. 6. Fantasia. I. Título. II. Série.

2025-606

CDD 028.5
CDU 82-93

Elaborado por Vagner Rodolfo da Silva - CRB-8/9410
Índice para catálogo sistemático:
1. Literatura infantojuvenil 028.5
2. Literatura infantojuvenil 82-93

Easier Classics
Alice's Adventures in Wonderland

Based on the original story by Lewis Carroll,
adapted by Gemma Barder.
Illustrations by Grace Westwood.

1st edition in 2025
www.cirandacultural.com.br

Alice's Adventures in Wonderland

Lewis Carroll

W. Books

Meet the Characters

Alice

The Hatter

The White Rabbit

The Queen of Hearts

The March Hare

The Duchess

Chapter 1

Alice sat in the shade of a tree at the bottom of her garden.

It was a warm, sunny afternoon. Alice's sister was reading a very boring book to her. It was so boring that Alice struggled to stay awake.

Just as Alice was about to fall asleep, she saw a white rabbit running past the tree.

It was a very **unusual** rabbit. It was running on two legs instead of four. It wore a smart red **waistcoat** and a tiny pair of glasses.

Alice checked her sister wasn't looking, then she ran after it.

She followed the rabbit through the garden gate and across the fields until it stopped.

unusual - *Strange, or something you wouldn't expect to see.*

waistcoat - *A smart button-up jacket without sleeves.*

Alice saw the rabbit take a silver **pocket watch** from its waistcoat pocket.

'Oh dear! Oh dear!' it said. 'I will be too late!'

Alice was very shocked to hear the rabbit talk. When she looked for the rabbit again, it had gone.

pocket watch - *A watch on a chain that is usually carried in a pocket.*

Alice searched for the rabbit and found a large **rabbit hole.** She knelt on the ground and looked down into it.

'Is there a rabbit in a waistcoat down there?' she called.

Suddenly, the soft ground underneath Alice fell away.

Down, down, down she fell into the **rabbit hole**.

rabbit hole - A place where rabbits live in small tunnels.

Suddenly - Quickly and not expected to happen.

Alice **tumbled** and **tumbled** down the hole.

It was getting brighter the further Alice fell. Now, she could see shelves on the wall. They were filled with candles, jars and lots of books.

Alice had been falling for so long that she became bored.

Down, down, down she fell into the tunnel.

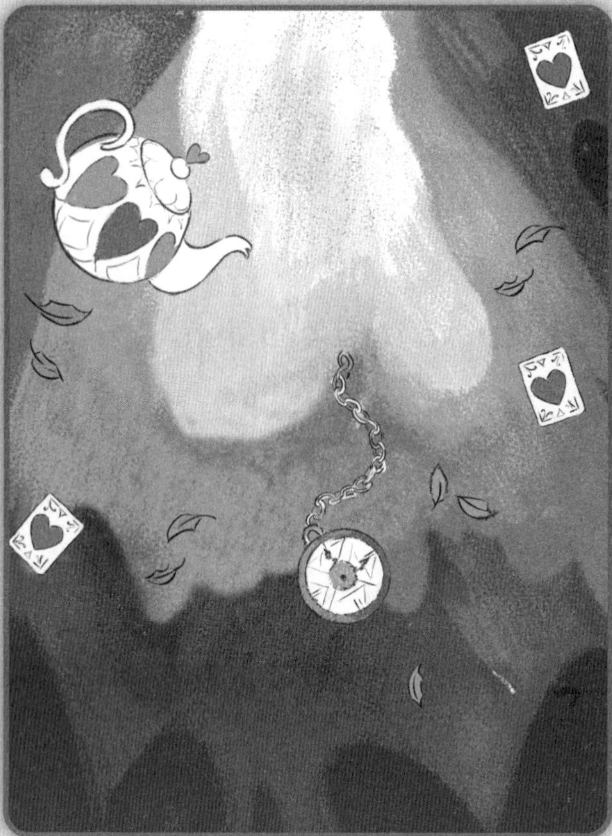

tumbled - *To suddenly trip or fall.*

Chapter 2

Finally, Alice landed with a bump on a pile of leaves.

She stood up and brushed the dirt off her light-blue dress.

She looked up into the tunnel that she had just fallen through. It was so long that she couldn't see the top!

Alice looked around.

She was in a long hallway with a black and white floor.

Along each side of the floor, were lots of doors.

Alice decided to try to open the doors.

She thought the doors might lead to a way out.

But each door was locked.

Just as Alice was about to try to climb back up the rabbit hole, she saw a glass table.

On top of the table was a tiny key and a blue glass bottle.

'A key!' Alice said. 'It must be for one of the doors!'

Alice tried to unlock each door, but the key was too small.

Alice sighed. She didn't know what to do.

Suddenly, she noticed a tiny door. It was the size of a **mousehole.** She thought the key must fit this door.

mousehole - *A hole or tunnel dug by a mouse.*

Alice knelt on the ground and looked through the tiny keyhole.

She saw a beautiful garden. This must be her way out!

She was much too big to fit through the door. But Alice remembered the little blue bottle on the table with a small label tied to it.

She picked up the bottle and read the small label. It said: *Drink me.*

Alice knew that drinking from the bottle wasn't a good idea because she didn't know what was inside the bottle.

But she decided to drink it because it might help her get home.

It tasted so **delicious** that she didn't notice she was **shrinking**!

delicious - *Something that tastes really good.*

shrinking - *Getting smaller.*

Chapter 3

Alice shrank so small that she could easily fit through the little door.

She rushed to the door and reached into her pocket for the tiny key. It wasn't there! Alice had left it on the table. The table that was now very tall.

As she began to cry, she saw a little box underneath the table.

Inside the box was a cake. In little raisins on top, it read: *Eat me.*

Alice picked it up. 'If the drink made me smaller, maybe the cake will make me big again!' she said. Alice tasted the cake. It was so delicious she ate it all!

When Alice had finished eating, she got quite a shock. She had grown and her head was touching the roof!

EAT ME

'Now I am far *too* big!' she said.

She picked up the tiny key and put it in her pocket.

She had no idea how she was going to fit through the little door now.

Alice heard footsteps. One of the doors opened and out came the White Rabbit.

The White Rabbit was holding a fan and a pair of white gloves.

'Oh dear,' said the rabbit. 'The Queen is going to be angry if I am late!'

'Excuse me!' said Alice from her tall height.

The rabbit was so scared that when he saw her, he dropped his fan and his gloves. He quickly ran to the little door.

The White Rabbit unlocked the door with his own key. He ran through the door and locked it on the other side.

Alice felt sad that the rabbit had left her. She began to cry. Huge teardrops splashed onto the floor.

Alice closed her eyes and used the rabbit's fan to cool her face. When she opened her eyes, she found she was up to her waist in water!

Chapter 4

Using the fan had made Alice shrink!

She was now so small that her puddle of tears was like a huge lake. She was going to have to swim.

As she began swimming, she noticed a mouse next to her. The mouse looked angry. Alice said she was sorry about all of the water. Together, they swam towards the door.

Finally, Alice and the mouse bumped into the little door.

Alice reached into her pocket for the key. She twisted the key in the keyhole.

As she pushed open the door, the water splashed out, carrying Alice and the mouse with it.

Alice looked around her. The garden was beautiful. Colourful flowers grew everywhere. They were taller than Alice and smelt sweet.

Alice turned to look for the mouse but it had already run away.

She was alone again.

Alice was looking around the garden when she noticed the White Rabbit.

'It's you!' Alice shouted happily.

'Mary Ann? What are you doing here?' asked the rabbit. 'Go home and fetch me a new pair of gloves and a fan.'

Alice realised that the rabbit was calling *her* Mary Ann. He had gotten her name wrong.

Chapter 5

'I'm not Mary Ann,' said Alice.

'We don't have time for this, Mary Ann!' said the rabbit. 'The Queen will be angry with me if I am late. Go!'

The rabbit began **shooing** Alice down the garden path with his little white paws.

shooing - *When someone waves their arms to make another person go away.*

Alice had no choice but to do what she was told.

After a short walk down the path, she came to a **rabbit-sized** cottage.

She was still very small, so she pushed the front door open and walked inside.

rabbit-sized - *The size of a rabbit.*

Alice went into the kitchen.

On the kitchen table, she saw a blue bottle. It looked the same as the blue bottle that had caused her to shrink. Except this bottle had no label.

She had a small sip. But this time she didn't shrink, she *grew*!

She grew until one leg stuck out of the front door of the cottage and one leg stuck out of the back door. Each arm was stuck out of a window!

'Oh dear,' sighed Alice.

Alice was stuck! She saw the White Rabbit hopping towards her.
He looked angry.

'What have you done?' asked the rabbit.

Before Alice could answer, the rabbit **burrowed** in the flowers next to the cottage. He then hopped out and began throwing pebbles at Alice.

'Please stop throwing pebbles at me!' called Alice.

The rabbit **rolled his eyes** and threw one into Alice's hands.

She looked closer. They weren't pebbles, they were small cakes!

burrowed - *Dug a hole or tunnel.*

rolled his eyes - *When someone moves their eyes in a circle to show they are not happy.*

Alice nibbled on the cake.

This was difficult since her arms were hanging out of windows and her head was in the attic!

She began shrinking again.

Once she was small again, she ran out of the house.

The White Rabbit had gone.

Alice felt sad. She wanted to fix the rabbit's house for him but didn't know where to start.

Instead, she decided to carry on walking down the path.

She thought about how she would ever get out of this strange place.

Chapter 6

Alice had been walking down the path for a long time. She now found herself in the woods.

She noticed clouds of blue smoke further ahead. As she got closer, the smoke turned purple, then red, then orange.

Alice thought this was **curious**.

curious - *Strange or unusual.*

Soon, Alice found herself stood below a giant mushroom. On top sat a blue caterpillar smoking a **pipe**.

'Excuse me!' Alice called. 'Please can you help me?'

The Caterpillar turned slowly to look down at Alice.

'Whoo aaare youuu ...?' the Caterpillar asked slowly.

pipe - *An old-fashioned tool used for smoking.*

Alice had to think carefully about this.

'I have changed so much today. I have grown and shrunk. Now, I don't know who I am,' said Alice.

'Hooow silly,' he said. 'I know who I am.'

Alice thought the Caterpillar was being rude.

‘Well,’ Alice said **crossly**. ‘Maybe you won’t know who you are when you change into a butterfly!’

‘I will *always* know who I am,’ said the Caterpillar.

Alice sighed, ‘I just want to be the same size I was this morning. Changing size is confusing and being small is no fun.’

crossly - *A little bit angrily.*

The Caterpillar was small and he liked his size. He thought Alice was being mean so he started to crawl away.

'Just remember this,' he said. 'One side of the mushroom will help you grow and one side will help you shrink. Secondly, **keep your temper!'**

Then, he took his pipe and left.

keep your temper - *A warning to tell someone to be careful not to get too angry.*

Alice took a piece of the mushroom from *each* side.

She ate a bit of the mushroom from one side and shrank.

Eating the other side made her grow until her head was in the clouds!

She ate a bit of both until she was her usual size again. Then, she put the rest of the mushroom in her pocket.

Chapter 7

As Alice walked through the woods, she spotted a small cottage. She hoped that if someone was inside, they might be able to help her.

She was far too tall for the small house. She took a small nibble from the mushroom in her right pocket, shrinking until she was just the right size for the front door.

Before Alice knocked on the cottage door, she saw the strangest sight.

A smartly dressed fish walked to the front door on its tail. The fish knocked on the door. A short woman answered.

'**Duchess**, here is your invitation to play **croquet** with the Queen this afternoon! Don't be late!' said the fish, as bubbles popped out of its mouth.

Duchess - *A lady who is related to royalty.*

croquet - *An outdoor game where wooden sticks are used to hit wooden balls through hoops.*

Once the fish had left, Alice knocked on the door.

The Duchess answered again. This time, she was holding a small **bundle** in her arms, like a baby.

'Are you coming in or not?' said the Duchess.

Alice followed the Duchess into the kitchen. A cook was adding lots of pepper to all the food on the hob.

bundle - *Something that is wrapped up.*

Warming itself by the stove, sat a beautiful cat that seemed to be smiling.

'Why is your cat smiling?' asked Alice.

'Because he's a Cheshire cat. All Cheshire cats smile like that,' **explained** the Duchess.

explained - *To help someone understand.*

'Here, you hold Pig. I need to get ready for croquet with my sister!' said the Duchess, handing Alice the bundle.

Alice thought *Pig* was a strange name for a baby, until she looked down at the bundle. She realised she was actually holding a **piglet.**

Alice carried the **piglet** out into the woods and placed it on the floor. It nodded at Alice before running away.

piglet - *A baby pig.*

Chapter 8

Alice decided not to go back into the Duchess's house.

'Can I help?' said a voice. It was the Cheshire Cat.

The cat was now sitting in a tree in the woods.

'I am wondering which way I should go,' said Alice.

The cat pointed his paw towards one path and said, 'The Hatter lives that way.' Then, it pointed his paw at the other path. 'The March Hare lives that way. They are both mad!'

Alice was confused. She thought it was rude to call someone "mad".

'How do you know they are mad?' she asked.

'Because we are all mad here!' said the cat as it **disappeared**. She had never seen a **disappearing** cat before!

Alice decided to walk down the path towards the March Hare.

disappeared / disappearing - *Went away.*

‘One more thing!’ said the cat, **reappearing** in front of Alice, making her jump with surprise. ‘Will you be playing croquet with the Queen?’

Alice smiled. ‘I would love to! But I haven’t been invited,’ she said.

The cat then disappeared, leaving only its smile behind. Slowly, even its smile **vanished** too.

‘How curious!’ said Alice.

reappearing - *Came back.*

vanished - *Went away completely.*

After the Cheshire Cat had vanished, Alice carried on walking down the path until she saw another little house.

She could hear singing and laughing.

It sounded as if someone was having a party...

Chapter 9

Alice arrived at a large dining table in a garden. It was covered with sandwiches, cakes and tea.

At one end of the table sat the March Hare. Next to him, was a man in a tall green hat.

Alice guessed he was the Hatter.

Between them was a dormouse fast asleep on a raisin bun.

Trying not to disturb anyone, Alice sat down at the table.

‘Who asked you to sit down?’ asked the March Hare.

Alice had no answer. She was hungry and tired, so she stayed sitting there.

‘It’s okay,’ called the Hatter. ‘You can have some tea if you answer a simple **riddle**.’

riddle - *A spoken puzzle that needs to be solved.*

Alice clapped her hands. She loved riddles!

'Why is a raven like a writing desk?' asked the Hatter.

Alice thought about it.

She was usually good at riddles, but this one was difficult.

The Hatter sighed and pulled out his pocket watch.

'Now!' he said. 'Back to the most important thing, my watch.

We've tried spreading butter on it and dipping it in tea, but nothing works. It still says six o'clock.'

The dormouse suddenly woke from her sleep.

'Six o'clock?' she squeaked. 'Everybody switch!'

The March Hare, the Hatter and dormouse all got up from their seats and quickly moved three spaces down the table.

They all looked at Alice.

Alice smiled.

'I understand what you are doing!' she said. 'The hatter's watch is broken and it always says six o'clock. That means it is always tea time.'

'Very clever!' said the Hatter.

'At six o'clock, everyone has to move around the table to get fresh tea and cakes. That's why there's no room at the table!' Alice said **proudly**.

proudly - *The way someone does something when they are happy with their choices.*

'Very good!' said the Hatter.

'Thank you,' said Alice. 'Can you tell me the answer to your riddle now?'

'I cannot. *I* don't even know the answer!' replied the Hatter.

Alice was getting very angry. Then, she saw a door in a tree trunk nearby.

'Thank you,' she said. 'But I'll be leaving now.'

Chapter 10

Alice stepped through the door in the tree and found herself in a beautiful garden. It was filled with red rose bushes.

She wandered through the garden, looking at the pretty roses. She reached out to touch a petal.

'What are you doing?' said a voice from behind the bushes.

The voice came from a **playing card**, a talking **playing card**! It was as tall as Alice and was holding a dripping paintbrush.

'Are you *painting* the roses?' asked Alice who couldn't believe what she was seeing.

playing card - *A small card with numbers on it, used for playing games.*

Just then, another playing card came rushing towards them carrying a tin of red paint.

'Seven! The Queen will be here soon and we haven't finished!' said the card.

'I know, Four,' said Seven. 'And this little girl has touched the roses we've already painted! She's smudged one.'

Alice felt bad for ruining Four and Seven's work.

'*Why* are you painting the roses?' asked Alice, feeling confused.

Four checked that no one was listening.

He whispered, 'The Queen only wants *red* roses in her garden. But we accidentally planted a row of *white* roses. We need to paint them all red before the Queen sees them.'

‘Or what?’ asked Alice.

‘Or it is **off with our heads**!’ replied Seven.

Alice laughed **nervously** and said, ‘Surely the Queen wouldn’t cut off your heads for a little mistake!’

‘She would,’ said Four. ‘We need to hurry, or else.’

off with our heads - *An order that comes from a king or queen to take off somebody's head.*
nervously - *The way someone does something when they feel scared or worried.*

Seeing how scared the playing cards were, Alice found a spare paintbrush and started to paint the roses red.

As they finished the last rose, a **trumpet sounded** and marching feet could be heard coming towards them.

'The Queen!' cried Seven, hiding the paint tins and brushes.
'She's coming!'

trumpet sounded - *A trumpet is played to announce the arrival of royalty or an army.*

Chapter 11

A **procession** of playing cards marched like soldiers past Alice, Four and Seven.

At the very end of the **procession**, was the Queen of Hearts herself, being carried on a golden throne.

The Queen of Hearts wore a dress covered in hearts, a large crown on her head and a **scowl** on her face.

procession - *A group of people, animals or cars moving forward in an organised way.*

scowl - *An angry frown on a person's face.*

Alice **stood to attention** like she had seen soldiers do when someone important walked past.

'Wait!' shouted the Queen. 'Put me down!'

The Queen climbed off of her throne, bent down and sniffed the painted rosebushes behind Alice.

stood to attention - *When people stand straight with their feet together and their arms by their sides.*

The Queen picked one of the roses and looked at it closely. A trickle of red paint dripped onto her hand.

'These roses have been *painted*!' she shouted. '**Page**! Get here at once!'

Alice was surprised to see the White Rabbit hopping towards the Queen.

'What can I do for you, Your **Majesty**?' asked the rabbit.

Page - *A young person that looks after a king or queen.*

Majesty - *The word you call someone with power like a king or a queen.*

‘Four and Seven have been *painting* roses! Off with their heads!’ shouted the Queen.

‘Oh, but you can’t!’ squealed Alice. The Queen of Hearts turned and scowled at Alice.

‘How *dare* you tell me what I *can* and can’t do! Off with *your* head too!’ ordered the Queen.

Alice did not want to lose her head!

'Your Majesty,' said the White Rabbit. 'The girl is just a child. Perhaps she can keep her head if she learns how to behave?'

The Queen looked at Alice.

'Hmm, you are right,' she replied. 'She can join us for croquet instead. The game might teach her some manners!'

The Queen turned and climbed back onto her throne. She didn't notice the White Rabbit shooing away Four and Seven to hide behind a bush.

'Have Four and Seven lost their heads?' shouted the Queen.

'Oh yes, Your Majesty!' lied the rabbit.

Alice breathed a **sigh of relief**.

sigh of relief - *To relax because something you were worrying or frightened about is not a problem anymore.*

Chapter 12

Alice smiled at the White Rabbit. She was happy that he had saved Four and Seven from losing their heads.

'Mary Ann, what are you doing here?' the rabbit whispered.

He still thought her name was Mary Ann. Alice decided not to correct him. He seemed very busy with the Queen.

'I am trying to find my way home,' Alice said.

'Well, you will need to play croquet first,' he replied. 'If the Queen has asked you, then you really must.'

Alice and the rabbit followed the procession. They came to a green lawn that had been set up for a game of croquet.

'Is the Duchess here?' Alice asked the rabbit.

'Oh no, the Queen has put her in prison,' replied the rabbit. 'They argued over which flamingo they were going to use.'

'Flamingo?' Alice asked, confused.

'Shhh, Mary Ann. The game is about to begin,' whispered the rabbit **sternly**.

sternly - *When someone says something very seriously.*

Kings and queens from each **suit** were getting ready for the game. They were choosing which **mallet** and ball to play with.

As Alice stepped closer, she noticed that all the **mallets** were, in fact, flamingos.

The balls were actually rolled-up hedgehogs and the hoops were playing cards bent over into an arch.

suit - *The group that playing cards are put into, such as hearts and clubs.*

mallet/mallets - *A tool similar to a hammer, used to hit the ball through a hoop in croquet.*

'This is the most curious game of croquet I have *ever* seen!' said Alice.

As Alice watched, the game got *even* stranger!

Whenever a hedgehog was hit with a flamingo and looked as if it was about to go under a card, the card would move out of the way or the hedgehog would roll off in the wrong direction!

Alice lined up her flamingo's long neck with the hedgehog.

'I will try not to hit you very hard,' she whispered to the animals, feeling bad for them.

But *each* time she tried to hit the hedgehog, her flamingo would suddenly bend its head to look up at her, making it very difficult.

'What are you doing?' asked Alice.

The flamingo replied, 'Queen's orders.'

Alice had a feeling this game was not being played fairly, but she had no choice but to keep trying.

Chapter 13

As Alice carried on playing the game of croquet, she realised there was no way to win.

When she finally managed to hit a hedgehog, it was about to roll under a playing card, but the playing card fell flat. The hedgehog rolled straight over it!

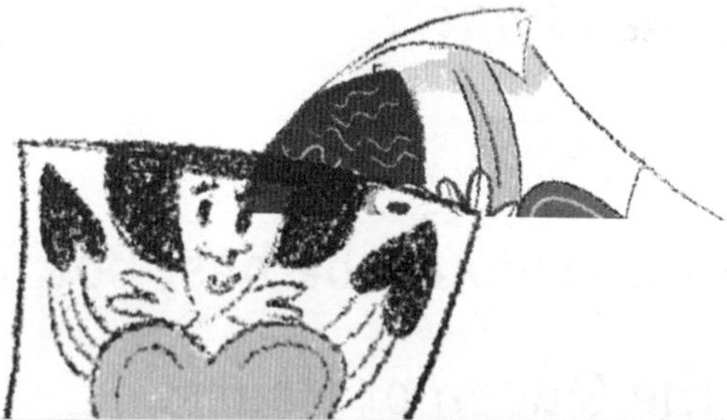

This game was unfair!

Alice could feel herself getting **cross**, until she remembered what the Caterpillar had told her.

Keep your temper.

She knew it would be best not to upset the Queen of Hearts.

cross - *When someone is a little bit angry.*

'Hello,' said a voice above Alice's head.

The Cheshire Cat **appeared**, curled up on a cloud, smiling.

'I see you were invited after all,' said the **floating** cat.

'I was. But I am not enjoying it,' Alice said.

appeared - *When something is seen that wasn't there before.*

floating - *To fly slowly in the air.*

Alice was just about to say that she thought the Queen was cheating. But, before Alice said anything, she had a feeling that the Queen was stood behind her.

Alice quickly changed her mind and lied, 'I think the Queen might be the best croquet player I have ever seen!'

The Queen walked past, smiling at Alice.

The King of Hearts followed the Queen as she walked across the lawn, watching the game.

'What is that?' asked the King, pointing at the Cheshire Cat floating in the air.

'It's a smiling cat, Your Majesty,' said Alice, wishing that the cat would disappear.

‘Why is it smiling? And why is it looking at *me*?’ said the King, getting very cross.

‘How dare you look the King of Hearts in the *eye*?’ said the King angrily.

‘A cat can look at a king,’ said the Cheshire Cat, who had begun to float above the King’s head.

The King became even more cross! 'Queen, I **demand** you order that this cat lose its head too!' shouted the King.

The Queen loved to give that order, so quickly **bellowed**, 'Off with its head!'

'Oh no, please don't hurt him,' said Alice.

demand - *When someone asks someone else to do something in a bossy and firm way.*

bellowed - *To shout loudly.*

'Don't worry Alice, the King and Queen can have my head,' said the cat. 'Look, here it is.'

The cat's body vanished, leaving just his smiling face floating around.

The Queen opened her mouth to give an **order**, but no **order** came out.

How could she cut off someone's head when there was only a head in the first place?

order - *An instruction given from a person of power.*

Chapter 14

Once the Queen had realised that she couldn't cut the head off of a cat with no body, she grew tired and went back to her game.

Alice was starting to grow tired too. She was tired of the Queen and the strange place she had found herself in.

She wanted to go home.

‘**Trial**!’ shouted the White Rabbit. Everyone stopped their game and looked at him.

‘Now begins the **trial** of the **Knave** of Hearts!’

Alice wanted to learn more. She had never seen a **trial** in real life before.

Trial - *A way to find out if someone has broken the rules or not.*

Knave - *A young person that looks after a king or queen.*

'Oh, Mr Rabbit?' Alice called, hurrying along behind the rabbit. 'Who is the knave and what has he done wrong to be put on trial?'

'Mary Ann, I don't have time to explain,' said the rabbit in a hurry. 'You can come and watch if you'd like.'

Alice followed along. She wanted to see what a trial looked like in this strange land.

Alice followed the White Rabbit towards a large, important-looking building.

Inside, it looked like any other **courtroom** that Alice had read about.

There was a seat behind a large desk which **overlooked** two lines of smaller desks and rows and rows of seats.

courtroom - *A room where a trial takes place.*

overlooked - *A view from above.*

Alice silently took a seat and waited for the **judge**, who just so happened to be the Queen of Hearts herself.

'Bring in the prisoner!' the Queen shouted.

Out of a **trapdoor**, the Knave of Hearts appeared with a chain around him. Alice wondered what he could have done. It was probably something very bad.

judge - *A person who decides whether or not a person has broken the rules or the law.*

trapdoor - *A door in the floor.*

The White Rabbit began to read aloud from a **scroll** of paper.

'Knave of Hearts! You are **accused** of stealing twelve of Her Majesty's finest jam tarts!'

Alice was shocked! Jam tarts? What a small crime!

'I call our first **witness**,' said the rabbit. 'I call the Hatter!'

scroll - *A roll of paper.*

accused - *A person that has been put on trial because people think they have broken the rules.*

witness - *A person who sees an event or crime take place.*

Chapter 15

Alice remembered the Hatter as he took a seat on a tall stool in the courtroom.

They had met at the strange tea party. He was still wearing his tall green hat and holding the same teacup.

'Mr Hatter, what do you have to say?' said the King of Hearts, **pacing** in front of the Hatter's stool.

pacing - *Walking at a steady speed, back and forth.*

The Hatter looked very nervous.

'I think the March Hare said something to the dormouse about the tarts,' began the Hatter. 'But then the dormouse fell asleep and the hare bounced about. Nothing happened until Alice turned up.'

Alice felt her cheeks turn red with **embarrassment**. What did *she* have to do with the trial?

embarrassment - *Feeling uncomfortable or shy about something that has happened.*

‘But what about the tarts?’ asked the Queen.

‘Well,’ answered the Hatter. ‘The dormouse likes tarts, but only in winter. The March Hare is allergic to round things, so-’

‘Enough of this nonsense!’ shouted the Queen. ‘Next witness!’

The Hatter quickly left, drinking his tea as he walked away.

Alice remembered the next person. It was the Duchess's cook.

'Did you make the tarts?' asked the King, pacing the courtroom again.

'Yes. I made them with jam and pepper, just as the Queen likes them,' said the cook.

Alice remembered how much the cook liked to use pepper.

With everyone talking about tarts, Alice began to feel hungry.

She reached into her left pocket and found some of the Caterpillar's mushroom.

Alice was very hungry. She decided to have a tiny nibble of the mushroom.

‘And who do you think stole the tarts?’ the King asked the cook.

‘Well, I don’t know,’ the cook replied. ‘Maybe that young girl who stole the pig from us? What was her name? Alice!’

Chapter 16

At the mention of her name, Alice tried to hide behind the rows of seats. This was difficult because, after eating the mushroom, she was beginning to grow.

'I have made a decision!' said the Queen. 'Knave, you are free to go!'

Alice was happy the knave was free. She thought that the Queen was starting to realise she shouldn't put people in prison for stealing some jam tarts!

'Now, **seize** the girl called Alice and bring her to me!' shouted the Queen.

seize - *To suddenly grab something and hold it tightly.*

Alice jumped to her feet. But to her surprise, her head was now touching the courtroom roof!

'Make yourself shorter at once!' shouted the Queen.

Alice folded her arms and shouted, 'No!'

'Silence!' shouted the Queen. 'I am the Queen and I say you stole the tarts. Off with your head! Cards!'

Suddenly, rows and rows of playing cards all ran towards Alice.

But now, Alice was taller than the playing cards. After eating the mushroom, she was taller than everyone she had met since falling down the rabbit hole.

As the playing cards ran towards her, she simply pushed them away.

From a distance she heard the White Rabbit calling to her, 'Alice! Alice!'

Alice thought this was strange. The White Rabbit always called her "Mary Ann".

He carried on shouting, 'Alice! Wake up! You have been asleep for *such* a long time!'

Chapter 17

Alice blinked. Sunlight shone through the branches of trees.

'You fell asleep!' said Alice's sister.

'The Queen, the White Rabbit and the Hatter were all here,' replied Alice.

'You've been dreaming again, Alice,' said her sister. 'Come on, Mum will want us home for tea.'

Alice followed her sister back to the house. She was certain the White Rabbit would hop in front of her, or the Cheshire Cat's head would appear.

'It felt so real...' she said. 'It was very curious. It was a wonderland!'

'A whole wonderland?' said Alice's sister. 'That's the best dream you have ever had!'

Just then, Alice put her hands into the pocket of her dress. She felt something inside the right pocket.

It was the Caterpillar's mushroom! She still had the pieces!

Had it been real after all? She would only need to take a little bite to find out...

Lewis Carroll

In 1832, Lewis Carroll was born in Cheshire. When Carroll was young, he loved making games and stories for his family and friends. On a picnic with his friend and his children, Carroll had the idea to write *Alice's Adventures in Wonderland*. It became the most popular children's book in England.